MEGAN'S MASQUERADE
by Trisha Magraw

Illustrations by
Bill Dodge

Spot Illustrations by
Rich Grote and *Catherine Huerta*

MagicAttic
Club

MAGIC ATTIC PRESS

Published by Magic Attic Press.

Copyright ©1996 by MAGIC ATTIC PRESS

For more information contact:
Book Editor, Magic Attic Press, 866 Spring Street,
P.O. Box 9722, Portland, ME 04104-5022

First Edition
Printed in the United States of America
1 2 3 4 5 6 7 8 9 10

Magic Attic Club is a registered trademark.

Betsy Gould, Publisher
Marva Martin, Art Director
Robin Haywood, Managing Editor

Edited by Judit Bodnar
Designed by Susi Oberhelman

ISBN 1-57513-072-6

Magic Attic Club books are printed on acid-free, recycled paper.

As members of the
MAGIC ATTIC CLUB,
we promise to
be best friends,
share all of our adventures in the attic,
use our imaginations,
have lots of fun together,
and remember—the real magic is in us.

Alison *Keisha*

Heather *Megan*

Contents

Chapter 1
A Surprise Announcement
7

Chapter 2
A Trip to the Past
15

Chapter 3
The Masquerade Ball
27

Chapter 4
Another Visitor
35

Chapter 5
Master Ryder
41

Chapter 6
The Journey Begins
49

Chapter 7
Traitors!
57

Chapter 8
The Return Trip
67

Megan's Diary Note 73

Learn More About It 76

Chapter

One

A SURPRISE ANNOUNCEMENT

P lease put away your math books, class," Ms. Austin said. "I have an important announcement."

"Oh no," Alison McCann moaned. "Don't tell me it's another spelling test."

Megan Ryder couldn't help smiling at her friend's pained expression. "Maybe it's something good—like a class trip or a school play," she said hopefully.

"Or a day off from school," Noah Cummings added. "Wouldn't—"

"Shhh!" Megan motioned for Noah and Alison to be quiet as Ms. Austin started talking again.

"As all of you know," the teacher was saying, "we've been talking about many important people and events from history this year. This afternoon we're going to begin discussing our own histories."

"Our own histories?" Keisha Vance repeated. "What does that mean?"

"Maybe you've never thought of your own life this way, Keisha," Ms. Austin explained. "But we're all a part of history. Each of us living now, at the end of the twentieth century, is a part of what's happening in the world around us. And years from now, future generations will look to us to tell them about our times."

Megan saw a smile flicker across the teacher's face. "That's why we're going to leave them some artifacts," Ms. Austin added mysteriously.

"Aren't artifacts the clues that archaeologists find when they're exploring ancient ruins, or digging up fossils?" asked Linda Chang.

Ms. Austin nodded. "That's exactly what they are, Linda—clues about the past. We're going to put our artifacts in a time capsule."

"A time capsule?" Megan blurted out. "That's a great idea!" She had read about people making time capsules and burying them underground, but she never thought she'd have the chance to make one herself.

"I think it's a great idea, too, Megan," Ms. Austin said. "Each one of us is going to place something in the time capsule before we bury it in the schoolyard. It should be an object that says something about you personally, and something about the times in which we live."

This is going to be so much fun, Megan thought as Ms. Austin started writing on the blackboard. She almost always enjoyed working on class projects, but this one sounded especially interesting. Just as Ms. Austin had said, it was a chance to be a part of history.

Several students let out groans as Ms. Austin wrote the word *Homework* on the board.

"Homework on the weekend?" complained Noah.

"Don't worry," Ms. Austin replied, turning back to face the class. "Your assignment is an easy one. I just want you to think about what I've said, and then decide what your artifact is going to be. On Monday, we can start putting our time capsule together."

"Ms. Austin! Ms. Austin!"

Heather Hardin rolled her eyes at Megan as Joey Diaz, one of the class clowns, shot his hand in the air and tried to get the teacher's attention.

"I already know what I want to bury underground," he

burst out. "My brother Robert's smelly sweat socks!"

A couple of the kids laughed, but Ms. Austin only shook her head. "I hope you can come up with something better than that, Joey," she said.

Megan hoped Joey could, too. She wanted their time capsule to be really interesting, not just filled with silly things that wouldn't mean anything to future generations. As the bell rang, ending school for the week, Megan's own mind was already churning with ideas.

"So what are you going to put in the time capsule?" Megan asked Alison a short while later as she and her three best friends sat in her spacious kitchen after school. It was still early fall, but the afternoon had turned gray and chilly, and the four girls were warming themselves with cups of steaming hot chocolate.

Alison's blue eyes sparkled with excitement. "A program from the summer Olympics," she announced proudly.

"That's a great idea, Ali," Keisha told her.

"It sure is," Heather agreed. "My mom told me that the Olympic Games started a long time ago, back in ancient Greece. They're really a part of history—*world* history."

"I'm thinking about putting in one of my family's Kwanzaa candles," Keisha said. "Or maybe an old Munchkins' record."

Megan grinned. "Last week my aunt was playing some of her old records—you should have seen her dancing to this song by the Monkees called 'The Last Train to Clarksville'!"

The friends groaned in unison.

Heather spooned some of the marshmallows off the top of her cocoa and popped one into her mouth. "I might draw a picture of our school so that the kids who find the time capsule can see exactly what it used to look like."

"That's a good idea, too," Megan remarked. She was really impressed. Each of her friends had come up with an interesting and different suggestion for the time capsule.

"What about you, Megan?" Heather asked. "Have you thought of anything yet?"

"I bet she has," Alison jumped in. "And I bet it's a book!"

The others smiled at Alison's guess. Megan spent nearly every free minute with her nose in a book. When she wasn't reading new books by her favorite authors, or rereading classics like A Wrinkle in Time, she was sitting at her desk, writing in her diary.

"I did think of putting a copy of Little Women or Harriet the Spy in the time capsule," Megan admitted as her cat,

Ginger, hopped into her basket. "But now I'm not sure those are good artifacts."

Keisha looked surprised. "Why not?" she asked.

"Well, for one thing, they're old books," Megan told her. "I want my artifact to be something that really is about now." She paused, thoughtfully stroking Ginger's soft orange fur. "I even thought about a page from my diary, but I don't think anybody in the future would really care about my private thoughts. I'll just have to figure out something else by Monday morning."

"If I know you, Megan," Keisha said confidently, "you'll have come up with a great artifact *before* Monday morning."

Chapter Two

A TRIP TO THE PAST

After her friends had gone home, Megan poked her head in the family room. Her aunt was sprawled on the couch, intently reading a colorful brochure.

"Hi Aunt Frances," Megan said. "What's up?"

Her aunt smiled brightly. "'Up', my dear niece, is exactly the right word."

"Excuse me?" Megan said as Aunt Frances sat up and waved the brochure at her.

"You'll never believe this, Megs," she went on. "I'm

going hot-air ballooning this weekend!"

"Actually, I do believe it," Megan replied with a smile. Her aunt had come to live with Megan and her mother shortly after Megan's parents' divorce. One of the best parts about having Aunt Frances around was that Megan got to hear about all of her many adventures, including her recent kayaking trip through treacherous rapids.

"Just think," Aunt Frances went on in a dreamy tone, "tomorrow afternoon, I'll be soaring through the blue sky, miles above our town, over the mall, the post office . . . Whoops." She glanced sheepishly at Megan. "I was so excited about the balloon ride, I almost forgot to tell you. There's a letter on your desk. It's from—"

Megan took off for the stairs before Aunt Frances could finish what she was saying. As she burst through the door of her room, she immediately spotted the overnight letter lying on top of her desk. Just as Megan had hoped, the letter was postmarked "South America" and it was from her father.

Megan's father was a foreign correspondent for a news magazine who traveled all over the world. For the last month he had been in South America, covering an important political election.

Megan eagerly tore open the envelope and pulled out the letter. As she dropped onto her bed, she began reading.

A Trip to the Past

Dear Megan,

This is just a short note to say I miss you and to let you know that I'm hoping to be in town this weekend.

"This weekend—all right!" Megan exclaimed happily. She was glad her father kept in close touch by sending letters and postcards, but she was thrilled when she got to see him in person. She turned back to the letter:

It's been an exciting time to be in South America. I've interviewed nearly all the candidates running for office, and I feel as though I'm watching history in the making. More details when I see you. I'll take you to dinner on Saturday night at Le Jardin, our favorite French restaurant.

In the meantime, I hope you're still keeping that diary of yours, and recording all your thoughts and observations about the world— just like a true writer!

Love,
Dad

My father has the best job, Megan thought as she reread what he had written about the elections. He was always meeting famous people and playing a part in important things happening all around the world. Megan wasn't sure what she wanted to do when she was older, but she hoped it would involve traveling to foreign countries, the way her dad's job did, and maybe involve writing, too.

Dad will be really interested in the time capsule project, Megan thought as she flopped back onto her bed. And now I'll get to tell him about it in person.

Megan spent the next morning helping her mother with chores. After that, she roamed aimlessly around the house, trying to think of something to do. Her father wasn't due until dinnertime, and Keisha, Alison, and Heather were all busy doing things with their families.

"Is it okay if I go to Ellie's for awhile, Mom?" she asked after lunch.

"Sure." Her mother lowered the newspaper she was reading and smiled at Megan. "Just make sure you're back in time for dinner with your dad."

"No problem," Megan said. She pulled on her jacket, gave her mom a quick kiss, then hurried out the door and down the street.

A Trip to the Past

Sometimes it seemed to Megan that she and her three best friends spent more time at Ellie Goodwin's house than they did at their own homes. The older woman had traveled all over the world, and the girls loved exploring her attic, which was filled with fascinating mementoes from her trips. They especially loved sifting through the old steamer trunk in the attic; whenever they tried on one of the outfits and looked into the tall, gilt-edge mirror next to it, they found themselves in the middle of an exciting adventure. Megan couldn't wait to see where her next trip would take her.

As Megan knocked on Ellie's door, she could hear piano music drifting through the house. Ellie had retired from her career as a performer several years before, and now she gave music and dance lessons in her home.

Megan had just decided to turn around and go home when the door opened. Ellie stood in the entryway dressed in a brightly colored knit sweater and a blue skirt that matched the color of her sparkling eyes.

"Why, Megan," Ellie said, smiling warmly as she held open the door. "Come on in."

Megan hesitated, feeling a little embarrassed. "I didn't realize you had a lesson this afternoon, Ellie," she began to apologize. "I'll come back later when you're—"

"Nonsense," Ellie interrupted. She ushered Megan into

the front hallway. "You know you're welcome here any time you like." She waved a hand at her surroundings. "Just make yourself at home, dear," she added. "I'll be finished shortly."

Megan thanked Ellie, then tiptoed past the living room where Ellie gave her lessons and headed for the sitting room. She loved nearly every room in Ellie's white Victorian house, but after the attic, the sitting room was her absolute favorite. The walls were decorated with interesting framed photos and posters, and books of all sizes lined the far wall. Whenever she entered the cozy room, she felt like curling up on the sofa in front of the fireplace and reading for hours.

Megan went over to the bookcase and gazed up at the crowded shelves. As she searched for something to read, a handsome leather-bound volume caught her eye. It was a dark green book with gold lettering along the spine: *The Great Depression* by Paul Theodore Ryder.

She repeated the author's name out loud. Excitement rippled through Megan as she reached for the book. Paul Theodore Ryder was her father's grandfather, Megan's great-grandfather, who had written several books about American history. Megan could still picture Great Paul's lively green eyes and hear his booming laugh when he used to read to her and tell her stories about the past.

Unexpectedly, a lump rose in Megan's throat. Now Great Paul was very old and very ill. She lingered over that thought a few moments and was about to open his book to the first chapter, but her mind suddenly turned to Ellie's attic.

Absent-mindly tucking Great Paul's book under her arm, Megan turned around and headed for the entry hall. As she reached into the silver box where Ellie kept the attic key, she could hear Ellie's student playing a sweet, clear melody.

Megan scooped up the key and hurried upstairs to the second floor. She slid the key into the lock and climbed up the next flight of stairs to the attic. Outside the wind was banging the shutters against the house and sending dry leaves skittering across the ground below. The late-afternoon sun streamed in from the high dormer windows, filling the room with rose-colored light.

Megan felt an immediate calm and walked over to the antique steamer trunk. Every time she opened it, she was surprised to find wonderful clothes that she didn't remember seeing the time before. Today the trunk overflowed with a magician's cape, a beautiful party dress, and a red satin tuxedo with matching sequined shoes.

As Megan began her search, a flash of color caught her eye. It was a harlequin-checked dress with an explosion of red, orange, and pink. Ruffled lace peeked out from beneath the skirt, and a pair of jet-black shoes lay beside the gown.

Megan pulled the brightly colored dress out of the trunk. As she unfolded its long, billowy skirt, something fluttered to the floor. It was a black satin mask cut in a fancy shape, with sparkling red rhinestones in each corner.

Intrigued, Megan put up her long hair and tried on the mask. She giggled as she caught a quick glimpse of her masked reflection in the mirror.

Nobody would recognize me, she thought, not even my own best friends.

Megan kicked off her sneakers and slipped on the gown and black flats. She finished dressing and hurried over to the mirror, the mask in her hand.

When Megan peered through the eyeholes a moment later, she found herself standing on a wide, pillared porch of an old mansion. In front of the house, people in festive party attire were emerging from horse-drawn carriages.

Several women approaching the brick house wore colorful gowns like Megan's. Some of the men had on old-fashioned military uniforms while others sported brocade vests with ruffled white shirts and buckled shoes. Almost everyone wore fancy masks, much like Megan's.

Where am I? Megan wondered, when a voice startled her.

"Good afternoon, miss."

Megan jumped as a gray-haired gentleman beckoned for her to come over to where he and a woman stood greeting guests. From behind his sequined mask, Megan could see a pair of brown eyes gazing at her. "Welcome to Wide Hall," the man said. "I don't recognize you, miss, but that's part of the fun!"

The dark-haired woman beside him was dressed in a long, yellow gown and a mask decorated with delicate pearls. "We're delighted you could come to our masquerade ball," she added warmly.

Masquerade ball! As Megan smiled at the couple, she hoped that her own mask concealed at least some of her surprise at finding herself at a masked ball somewhere in the past!

How exciting, Megan thought as she followed the other guests into the mansion. On a table in a grand hallway, Megan spotted a letter with a brief address: *Mr. and Mrs. Clinton Little, Wide Hall Estates*. There was no stamp and no postmark, just a broken wax seal where the letter had been opened. Next to the seal someone had written the date, 1781.

1781!

That's when the American colonists were fighting for independence from England, Megan realized.

As she followed the other guests to the ballroom, an excited shiver traveled up Megan's spine. She was about to find out what it was like to live during the Revolutionary War!

Chapter Three

THE MASQUERADE BALL

egan's eyes widened as she entered an elegant ballroom. Windows stretched from floor to ceiling, and a huge chandelier filled with burning candles hung from the center of the room. In one corner stood a small group of musicians playing stringed instruments. Megan inhaled the scent of perfume and burning wax as she looked around the room.

A man in a worn brown military uniform noticed Megan and nodded politely. Megan shyly smiled back at him. She wondered if he was one of the famous figures from the Revolutionary War that she'd learned about at school. Maybe even George Washington was here, she thought, scanning the room, or Benjamin Franklin!

"How thoughtful of the Littles to hold such a gathering!" A woman's voice drew Megan's attention.

"It's been such a long and troubling war," the woman went on, addressing the man standing beside her. She poured herself a cup of tea from a tall silver pot. "But now that the horrible Englishman, Colonel Banastre Tarleton, has been driven back, we have something to celebrate. This ball is the perfect way to do it."

The man scowled at the mention of the colonel. "Tarleton came close enough to give us quite a scare," he said. "Burned my neighbors' fields and raided everyone's livestock. We're lucky he didn't massacre every one of us along his bloody route. Yes, indeed," the man added. "I think we all need a fine celebration to lift our spirits."

"I'm so glad it's a masked ball, too," said the woman. "So much more entertaining than . . ."

Megan lost track of their conversation. She had never heard of Banastre Tarleton. But it sounded as if he'd just been defeated by the colonial forces.

Suddenly she caught a few more words the couple was saying: ". . . our neighbor, Governor Thomas Jefferson."

Thomas Jefferson? Butterflies fluttered in Megan's stomach. They were talking about *the* Thomas Jefferson— the man who had been the governor of Virginia and later the president of the United States! Maybe she would get to see him, too!

"Would you care to dance?" a voice said suddenly. "I hate to see you standing here by yourself. This minuet is my favorite."

Megan turned to see a soldier with red hair and a stubble of beard standing before her. He was wearing a very plain military uniform.

"Y-y-yes, I'd love to," Megan said, caught off guard.

Megan followed the soldier to the middle of the room. I don't know what a minuet is, she thought nervously. How am I going to dance to it?

But to her relief, Megan soon found herself in perfect step with the red-headed soldier. After her trip through the attic mirror, she was able to bow to her partner as gracefully as everyone else in the room!

Megan quickly relaxed. Soon she was enjoying the rich, melodic notes of the stringed instruments and the swish of her long, billowing skirt as she danced around the ballroom. The other guests moved gently around

her, a colorful stream of
glittering sequins and
shimmering satin. Megan
couldn't help thinking
it was like being at a
Halloween party—it was
scary and exciting at the same
time to see everyone in their masks

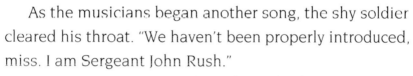

As the musicians began another song, the shy soldier
cleared his throat. "We haven't been properly introduced,
miss. I am Sergeant John Rush."

"My name is Megan Ryder," she replied. "Are you a
friend of the Littles?"

He shook his head. "Our company was passing Wide
Hall, looking for a pallet of straw to sleep on for the night
and the Littles insisted that we stay in more comfortable
quarters, have a good hot meal, and enjoy ourselves."

"So that's why some of the men are dressed in military
uniforms," Megan commented.

The soldier grinned. "I'm afraid most of us were too
busy fighting the Redcoats to properly prepare for a fine
masquerade ball."

"I'm sure the Littles don't mind," Megan said politely.
"Their home is lovely, isn't it?"

"That's for certain," the sergeant agreed. "Our hosts

are fortunate that Tarleton didn't burn it down before taking control of the governor's home, Monticello."

"What?" Megan blinked as she tried to remember some of the early American history she'd learned in school. "Colonel Tarleton took Thomas Jefferson's home?"

The sergeant nodded. "But don't you worry, Miss Ryder. The governor escaped with his staff hours before the enemy arrived. And just two days after the Redcoats moved into Monticello," he added, his eyes glowing proudly. "Our men drove them out. Hardly a thing was touched. Thanks to us, Monticello was spared."

Megan heaved a sigh of relief. "The colonial soldiers must be very brave," she replied. "Have you run into Colonel Tarleton yourself? He sounds like a dangerous man."

"I haven't," Sergeant Rush said. "But I know less fortunate who have." His voice cracked. "Trust me when I say that British monster has no respect for property or human life."

"Where is he now?" Megan asked.

"After the raid on Monticello, Tarleton retreated. How

far, I don't know." The soldier's expression brightened. "But let's talk of more pleasant things. Everyone is preparing to celebrate our country's independence next month, on July Fourth. I prefer to think ahead to victory and celebration."

"July Fourth?" Megan's eyes widened with surprise. "But the war won't end until . . ." She stopped herself just in time. She hadn't realized that Independence Day existed even before the end of the war.

"Until when?" the sergeant asked her, a quizzical expression on his face.

Megan wished she could tell the sergeant—and everyone else in the room—that their efforts would lead to victory. But she knew she couldn't. It would only get her into all sorts of trouble.

"Until our troops lead us to victory," Megan finished brightly, covering up her slip of the tongue.

Chapter

Four

ANOTHER
VISITOR

After several more dances, Megan thanked Sergeant
Rush, her partner, then poured herself a glass of
water from a pewter pitcher. As she stood on the sidelines
sipping the cool drink, her eyes followed a handsome couple
gracefully twirling around the room. The woman's long
blond hair was piled up high on her head behind a sparkling
tiara, and she wore a silver mask and a blue silk brocade
gown that shone like a polished jewel. Her tall partner was
dressed in a cream-colored ruffled shirt and a long, dark

jacket with large buttons. A white powdered wig covered his hair, and his embroidered mask concealed much of his face, except his dark eyes, which didn't leave the woman's face.

As Megan watched the pair dance together, she wondered who they were. Maybe they're husband and wife, she thought. Or maybe they're strangers who met today at the ball and fell in love!

When the music stopped a few minutes later, Megan made her way to a long table loaded with huge, delicious-smelling roasts and heaping platters of vegetables.

Megan was about to fill a plate when she spotted a girl about her age at a side door. She had long, dark hair and wore a simple cotton dress instead of a ball gown. The girl nervously scanned the room, her cheeks flushed with color.

Intrigued, Megan watched her for a few minutes. Obviously, she was looking for someone—but who, Megan wondered, and why did she look so nervous?

Finally Megan approached the girl.

"Oh, please don't tell on me!" the girl pleaded, looking like a frightened rabbit. "I desperately need to find someone."

"I'm not going to stop you," Megan said kindly. "In fact I'm a stranger here myself. My name is Megan Ryder."

Just then, the host, Mr. Little looked in their direction.

Megan saw the girl's eyes fill with panic. "No one must see me," she whispered.

"Here." Megan quickly scooped up a red shawl and fan that were lying on a chair, and thrust them at the girl. "These will help you blend in."

"Thank you," the girl murmured gratefully. As she wrapped the shawl around her shoulders, Megan led her into an empty room off the hallway.

Up close, Megan could see that the girl's face was smeared with dust, and dark circles ringed her eyes. "Are you all right?" she asked.

The girl nodded. "I'm fine, but I've traveled the back

37

roads all day, and I . . ." Her words trailed off.

"What is it?" Megan prodded her gently.

The girl hesitated for one more second. "I have to trust someone," she mumbled, more to herself than to Megan. She took a deep breath, then suddenly the words seemed to tumble out.

"My name is Sue Ellen Briggs, and my father is Jeb Briggs, an aide to Thomas Jefferson."

Megan listened carefully as Sue Ellen explained that her father had gone off with Jefferson several months ago. "He didn't want to go because of the new baby coming, but he said it was his duty to the country. Now I must find him to tell him about Mother," she added.

"Your mother had the baby?" Megan asked with concern. "Is she all right?"

Sue Ellen brightened. "She's very weak, but doing well, thank you. And so is my baby brother. He's chubby and adorable and has a whole head of hair." She took a handkerchief from her pocket. A "B" was embroidered in one corner of the neatly folded white lace. When Sue Ellen opened the handkerchief, Megan saw a fine dark curl of hair.

"It's for my father to keep with him while he's away from our family," Sue Ellen explained in a soft voice. Then her mood seemed to darken again as she added, "But it's not the only reason I must find him." Sue Ellen reached into her pocket again and this time she pulled out a piece of paper. A small seal of bright red wax held it closed.

Megan reached out to look at the seal more closely, but to her surprise, the girl snatched the paper away.

"I don't mean to be rude," Sue Ellen apologized, "but . . ." She leaned closer to Megan. "Can I trust you to keep a secret?"

"Of course," said Megan.

"The courier who brought this message was looking for Mr. Jefferson. He thought Mother might know where to find him because Father is one of his trusted aides. The messenger was shot by Redcoats," Sue Ellen went on. "Mother and I dressed his wound, but he had lost too much blood to travel farther. He told us that the letter is urgent—it comes from General Lafayette. Somehow, I must see that it reaches the governor."

A thrill raced through Megan. Sue Ellen was carrying a secret message for Thomas Jefferson! "Is it possible that your father is at the ball?" she asked.

"I was hoping to find him and Mr. Jefferson when I heard there was a large gathering here," Sue Ellen admitted. "But the room is so crowded, and so many people are wearing masks."

"There's a company of soldiers here," Megan told her. "Perhaps they can tell you where your father is."

"No!" Sue Ellen cried, shaking her head vehemently. "The courier said there are many spies and traitors in the army. He warned me to trust no soldiers with the message. And who knows if any of the other guests are trustworthy." She looked around. "I must return home soon. My mother is alone with the wounded messenger and the baby and she needs my help."

As Sue Ellen fell silent, Megan could hear gentle waltz music drifting out from the ballroom.

Poor Sue Ellen, Megan thought. Even though Megan's own father traveled a lot, she always knew where he was and how to get in touch with him. Sue Ellen's father's whereabouts were completely unknown—in the middle of a war. Maybe Mr. Briggs had been wounded—or worse, Megan thought grimly.

"I must get this message to the governor before returning home," Sue Ellen repeated in an urgent whisper.

"I'll do it." Megan said the words so suddenly that she surprised even herself. "I'll find a way to locate your father and Mr. Jefferson," she promised.

Chapter Five

MASTER RYDER

Y ou!" Sue Ellen exclaimed. She shook her head. "You're very kind, Megan, but how can you possibly get the message to Mr. Jefferson? You know less of him than I do."

"I'll mingle with the guests and soldiers," Megan replied. "Surely someone at the Littles' ball knows where he is."

Sue Ellen still looked uncertain.

"I'll be very careful, I swear. Now go home," she urged Sue Ellen. "Your mother needs you."

This time Sue Ellen gave in. "I don't know what else to do," she said, reluctantly handing over the sealed letter. "Thank you, Megan." She gave her a quick hug. "Please promise you'll send word when you hear something of Father and the governor."

"Of course," Megan replied. "Don't worry. You'll hear from me soon."

As Megan watched Sue Ellen leave, she felt a lot less sure of herself. What were you thinking? she chided herself. You don't even belong here. How could you have agreed to deliver a secret message to Thomas Jefferson?

Megan took a deep breath as she headed back into the ballroom. No matter how nervous she was, she had made Sue Ellen a promise, and she was going to keep it.

Through a window, Megan could see a small group of soldiers gathered on the veranda. They were chatting with some men dressed in tight leggings and fringed jackets. From what she remembered from pictures in her American history textbook, she guessed that these men were the military scouts whose job it was to blaze trails in the wilderness for the soldiers and be on the lookout for British Redcoats.

Placing her mask back over her face, Megan bravely walked out onto the porch. If anyone knew where to find Thomas Jefferson and Jeb Briggs, it would be these men.

Megan's palms felt damp as she stepped into the sunlight.

". . . British are planning a new assault," a soldier was saying.

"At least Monticello is safe," a scout joined in. "In fact, they say some of Jefferson's staff have ridden back to the estate to prepare for the governor's return."

The governor's return? Megan felt a burst of excitement. Maybe it would be easier to find Jefferson and Sue Ellen's father than she'd thought.

"You'd better hope you're right, Jason McCray," another voice replied.

Even though he was taller than most of the men around him, Megan figured Jason McCray was only a few years older than she was. Long, sandy brown hair fell in soft curls around his face and his steel blue eyes were sharp and piercing.

Jason laughed and threw back his head. "Well, it's my hide if I'm wrong!"

All of the men laughed, except the soldier who had spoken first. "Take heed," he warned. "There are traitors in our midst. You can't be too careful of anyone or of any information that is given to you."

Jason McCray's attitude grew more serious. "I'm sorry to say you're right, Martin. There are plenty of spies and traitors about—just remember Benedict Arnold."

Megan felt her heat beat faster. Benedict Arnold was another name she remembered from history—he was the solider who had betrayed the colonists to the British army!

"Every soldier and citizen despises Arnold," the man named Martin agreed. "How could a man who fought alongside George Washington assist the British?"

Megan couldn't hear Jason's response. But she could hear what he said next—he was leaving that evening for a two-day journey to Monticello.

Megan drew in her breath. Maybe she could persuade *him* to deliver the message to Jefferson and get word to Sue Ellen's father.

But a second later, Sue Ellen's words about the courier rang in her ears: *He warned me to trust no soldiers with the message.* Megan decided she'd better keep the message for Jefferson to herself.

She waited until Jason moved away from the group. Then she hurried toward him.

"Excuse me," she said, removing her mask. "My name is Megan Ryder. I heard you say you were going to Monticello. Please take me along."

"Take you to Monticello?" Jason stared at her, his

mouth agape. "Do you have any idea what you are asking of me, Miss Ryder?"

Megan nodded. "Yes, I do," she replied. "But I wouldn't dare make my request if it weren't a very urgent matter. There is someone there that I must see—a man named Jeb Briggs."

"What's your business with Jeb Briggs?" he asked suspiciously.

"His wife had a son," Megan replied. She quickly unwrapped the handkerchief and showed him the lock of baby hair.

"There's no need for you to travel all the way to Monticello, miss," Jason told her. "I'll gladly relay the news to Jeb Briggs myself."

Megan shook her head, thinking fast. "Please," she said finally. "His family won't rest until I come back with the news that he is well and has the baby's lock of hair."

Jason eyed her for another minute, then finally gave Megan a reluctant nod. "The war is very difficult on families," he acknowledged. "I'll take you to Monticello, Miss Ryder. But let me warn you, there is danger all about. Redcoat raiding parties are still in the region, and we

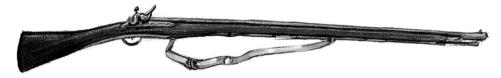

must travel on foot. The journey is long and difficult—
especially in a dress."

"I can manage it," Megan eagerly replied. "Though I
would like to change my clothes." For the first time since
she'd left home, she wished she had on her jeans and
sneakers instead of a long ball gown.

Suddenly a solution came to her. "I need a minute.
Please wait for me outside," she said, turning around and
dashing up the grand staircase.

On the second floor, Megan looked into open
doorways as she walked down the hallway. Thankful
that no one else seemed to be up there, she slipped

into a bedchamber at the end of
the hall. Hanging on a wooden
peg on the back of the door, was
exactly what she'd hoped to
find—a boy's britches, shirt, and
cloth jacket. They looked a little
big, but they would do.

Megan hid her gown in a trunk
at the foot of the four-poster bed,
praying that no one would discover
it or need the missing clothes
before she could return them.
Then she tucked the letter and Sue

Ellen's handkerchief into her pants pocket, grabbed a cap
from another peg, and headed downstairs.

Jason was waiting for her near the front porch. "You
are a speedy dresser, *Master* Ryder," Jason joked as Megan
stuffed her strawberry blond hair under her cap. He
handed her a pouch and a bedroll. "These are for
you. The nights are still mighty chilly." Megan slipped
the bedroll's rawhide straps through the loop in the
pouch and tied them around her waist. Jason picked up
his musket, with a wave to the men on the porch, he
led the way at a brisk walk.

The sun was beginning to set, and the air already
felt damp and chilly. As Megan pulled the worn cloth
jacket more tightly around herself, a frightening sound
rang out in the distance.

A gunshot, Megan realized nervously.

At the masquerade ball, Megan hadn't given the
war much thought. But now it dawned on her that
outside a real war was being fought with real enemies.

You'd better be careful, she told herself. She pulled
the cap lower over her eyes and followed the scout as
he entered the dark forest.

Chapter

Six

THE JOURNEY BEGINS

A short while later, Megan and Jason had to step off the rutted dirt road they were following to allow a wagon to pass. As it came up beside them, Megan gasped. In the dusky light, she could see that it was filled with wounded soldiers. They moaned in pain as the wagon bumped and rolled past. A few soldiers limped along behind, using branches or muskets for support.

A soldier with a shredded coat and a bloody bandage wrapped roughly around his head waved to Megan and

Jason from the back of the wagon. As Megan waved back, she found herself staring at the men in horror.

"Those poor soldiers," she murmured to Jason.

"Actually, those are the lucky ones," he said grimly. "They're on their way to the hospital. Some of them might die there," he admitted, "but it's a better fate than dying in the fields and along the roadways like so many other soldiers."

Those men were the lucky ones? Megan thought in disbelief. In school, she had thought about the American Revolution as a glorious time in the nation's history when men like Thomas Jefferson and George Washington led the colonies to victory. But after seeing the wounded men along the road, she realized that the war had been much harder and bloodier than she'd ever imagined. Even people like Sue Ellen and her family were forced to make sacrifices in the fight for freedom.

Megan was lost in thought until Jason spoke up. "Halfway to the river, we'll come to a cave that few people know about. We can rest there for the night."

"A cave?" Megan tried to sound brave, but it sounded so cold and damp.

Jason smiled. "It may not be the Littles' fine home, but it'll suit us until morning. It's well hidden," he explained. "And there's soft ground cover at the entrance where we'll be safe and warm."

Jason pulled out a long knife and began hacking away the branches of a large tree that blocked their path. "If we keep to a good, brisk walk, we'll be there in under an hour," he told her.

Megan climbed over the tree trunk, thinking how glad she was to have boots instead of dancing slippers. Even so, her feet felt blistered and her legs ached as Jason led her quietly but quickly through the woods. She wished she'd thought to bring something to eat and drink, but it was too late for that.

"Let me show you where we are and where we're going," Jason said when they reached a clearing. Megan expected him to take out a map showing Monticello. Instead, he pointed straight up.

The sky was ablaze with a blanket of stars. Megan had never seen the Milky Way so clearly. Its creamy white band made a bold sweep across the sky.

"Do you see the North Star?" Jason asked.

Megan nodded. The last star in the handle of the Little Dipper, bright and twinkling, stood out from the rest.

Jason went on. "This trip is a simple one—we only need to head due north. But when a person is out for days and weeks at a time in the wild, the stars are his

only guide." He paused, then added matter-of-factly, "I know the sky like the back of my hand."

Just then, a shooting star cut a swift and graceful path across the midnight blue sky.

"It's good luck," Megan said softly.

"I hope so," replied Jason. "Tomorrow should be an easier day. Once we reach the river, we're nearly there."

They trudged on until, just as Jason had promised, they came to a cave. It was nestled at the base of a rugged cliff surrounded by thick, protective woodland.

Megan looked around and sighed. "It's beautiful," she whispered. The night air had turned quite cold, but the quiet, moonlit night was so lovely that she was finally able to relax a little.

Jason seated himself on an outcropping of rocks, where he had a clear view of the area. "There's bread and cheese in that pouch. Care to open it up?" He reached into his own pack for a container of water.

"Would I!" Megan was ravenous. She quickly broke the food into four sections and handed a hunk of bread and a bit of hard white cheese to Jason and kept some for herself.

"This is our breakfast, too, remember," he added. Megan looked longingly at the rest as she put it back in the pouch.

The chewy brown bread wasn't as fresh and tasty as the meals Megan was used to, but she practically wolfed down the whole thick piece with her share of the cheese. After a drink from Jason's water skin, she felt more satisfied.

Megan lay down to rest her head on a pillow of moss. She tried not to think about how much she missed her comfortable, warm bed back at home or her worries about finding Jeb Briggs.

But it was a long time before her eyes closed and she fell asleep.

Jason woke Megan before the sun had cleared
the treetops. They drank the rest of the water, then
silently ate their rations as they began their trek
toward the river. By the time they finally reached it, the
sun was directly overhead. Every muscle in Megan's body
ached. The sips from the cool, running water tasted
delicious, especially with the small, plump blueberries
she and Jason picked for their lunch. The watercress
and wild lettuce they pulled from the shallows were
bitter, but Megan ate it all.

Jason urged her on the minute they'd finished eating.
"We must move even more quickly and carefully now,"
he insisted. "The closer we get to Monticello, the greater
the danger of running into Tarleton or an enemy patrol."

The misty Virginia morning had been quiet except for
the twittering of birds, and Megan had let herself forget
about the war and the possibility of Redcoats lurking in
the woods. She wished Jason hadn't reminded her now.

The two of them made their way through the
heavy undergrowth without speaking. Once or twice
Megan almost shared her secret about the message for
Thomas Jefferson with Jason, but each time she stopped
herself from speaking. Sue Ellen had said it was too
dangerous, she reminded herself.

She wiped the sweat from her forehead as she trudged

on beside Jason. The trek through the wild country was harder than she'd expected.

Jason gave her a sympathetic look. "Can you continue, Miss Ryder? We have less that an hour ahead of us now."

"I'm fine," Megan told him determinedly.

"Jeb Briggs's wife owes you a great thanks," Jason complimented her. "This is not an easy trip, even for an experienced scout."

Megan smiled and pushed on.

The afternoon was hot, and the sound of birds chirping seemed to stop. Occasionally the harsh call of a crow sounded nearby, and Megan saw a pair of buzzards circling above a clearing.

The next time Megan looked up, she saw a more alarming sight—smoke rising in the north, the direction of Monticello.

Chapter
Seven

TRAITORS!

ook, Jason!" Megan shouted, pointing to the smoke in the distance. All she could think of was what that man at the ball had said about the British burning down his neighbors' farms. "What if Tarleton is burning Monticello?" she asked him.

"Let's hope that's not the case," he said, gazing at the smoke in alarm. "But we'd better hurry."

Megan followed Jason as he picked up his pace through the low brush. What if they had come all this way only to find Jefferson's home burned to the ground? What if she wasn't able to find the governor to deliver the message from General Lafayette? What if she never found Sue Ellen's father? Panicked thoughts flooded her mind.

As Megan and Jason drew closer to the fire, the air was filled with an awful smell. A smoky haze drifted toward them, making both of them cough.

Jason tore his scarf in half, soaked it in water from his pouch, and handed half to Megan. "Tie this over your face," he instructed. "It will help."

With the scarf covering her nose and mouth, Megan could breathe more easily, but her eyes still burned. She reached up to rub them, then stopped when she saw that her hands were smudged with dirt and nicked with scratches and cuts.

"We'll wade along the river's edge as far as we can. The water will protect us from sparks and flash fires," Jason explained. "But farther down, there maybe copperheads in fallen branches and near the rocks, so be careful."

"You mean copperhead *snakes*?" Megan shuddered. The only snakes Megan had looked in the eye were at the local zoo. And those had been in cages!

"That's what I mean," replied Jason. "Are you all right?"

Megan took a deep breath. She was determined to keep going, no matter what. "I'm quite all right."

Traitors!

The river's dark, rippling water was icy cold and moving swiftly. The chill went right through Megan's boots, then crept up her britches. She remembered just in time to take the message and handkerchief from her pocket and slip them securely under her cap. Now and then she and Jason came upon rocky patches at the water's edge. She moved over them carefully, but they cut through her thick leather boots all the same.

When the wind changed direction at last and blew the fire the other way, Megan gladly took off her damp scarf and took big breaths of the fresh late-afternoon air. Up ahead, she could see a clearing where the river took a sharp turn. She followed Jason onto shore. Her skin tingled as she poured the water out of her boots. It felt great to be on dry land again.

Jason took a moment to get his bearings. When he realized the fire was burning to the east, he heaved a sigh of relief. "It's not Monticello after all," he murmured. "Jefferson's estate is that way," he added, pointing up a hilly incline.

The grass felt like a carpet under Megan's damp feet. She wanted to run all the way to Monticello. She started for the treeless path ahead.

"Keep to the tree line," Jason reminded her. "Anyone could spot us in the open."

But he spoke too late. Suddenly two soldiers rushed at them from a clump of bushes, holding out their bayonets.

"Halt!" cried the younger one, looking straight at Megan. She froze in her tracks, confused and trembling. Why were these soldiers, dressed in the uniform of the American colonists, stopping them?

"Make a move and you're dead!" the other soldier shouted, aiming his musket at Jason's head.

"But we're on your side," Megan protested.

"Hands up, I say," the first soldier shouted. Before Jason could say or do anything, the soldier grabbed Jason's musket and knife and shoved him with the butt of his own rifle, knocking him to the ground.

"Get up," snapped the soldier. He turned to his companion. "Spies or turncoats, no doubt." Then, picking his yellowed teeth with a dirty fingernail, he said to Jason, "You know what we do to traitors, don't you?"

"But you haven't let us explain," Megan protested.

Jason swayed dizzily as he got up. "We're also fighting

for freedom," he began. "We—"

The soldiers cut him off. "Our orders are to bring
in anyone we find nosing around this territory." When
Megan tried to wipe the blood from Jason's chin,
her guard slapped her hand down and spun her away.
The other soldier raised the sharp, gleaming tip of his
bayonet to Jason's neck.

Then Megan felt something sharp at the small
of her back.

"Now march!" growled a voice.

Megan's heart pounded as she and Jason walked ahead of their captors, their hands held high.

When they reached the crest of the hill, Megan drew in a breath at the sight below. "It's Monticello!" she exclaimed before she could stop herself.

Megan remembered learning that the name Monticello meant "little mountain" in Italian, and now she knew why. The grand estate rested on a grassy knoll. It was near dusk, and the building cast its long, distorted shadow over the ground. Its great white pillars and domed rotunda reflected the late afternoon light.

Something pressed hard against Megan's ribs, forcing her along a little faster. "How do you know this place?" her guard demanded suspiciously.

"I just heard about it," Megan answered, trying to cover her tracks. Luckily, her answer seemed to satisfy the soldier. But she knew she would have to be more careful next time.

When they neared the house, one of their captors grunted and pointed them to the back. "That's where we keep the dogs—and the traitors," he snarled.

I have to do something, and do it fast, Megan thought desperately. Just then she noticed a tall man standing on the porch.

"I must speak with Jeb Briggs," Megan demanded suddenly.

Megan's request brought gales of laughter from the two soldiers who had captured them. "Why surely," said one sarcastically. "I suppose you'd like to invite him for English tea."

"I'm here to tell Mr. Briggs that he's the father of a healthy boy," she said. Impulsively, she turned toward the porch and added in a loud tone, "And to deliver a message from General Lafayette to Thomas Jefferson."

Megan heard Jason's surprised gasp. Her secret was out.

"Tell us another one," exclaimed Megan's guard, laughing loudly.

But Megan's words had gotten the attention of the man on the porch. He bounded down the steps toward her. As he reached her side, Megan could see that he had dark hair and eyes—just like Sue Ellen's.

"What do you know of my wife and child?" Jeb Briggs demanded.

Megan removed her cap, and
her long hair tumbled down
her shoulders. Ignoring the
soldiers' startled reaction,
she carefully unfolded the
white handkerchief with the
embroidered "B" and showed the man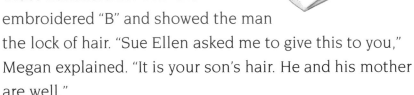
the lock of hair. "Sue Ellen asked me to give this to you,"
Megan explained. "It is your son's hair. He and his mother
are well."

"My son," Mr. Briggs repeated softly. He ran one finger
across the raised threads of the embroidery, then closed
his big hand around the soft lock of hair. "Thank you,
miss," he whispered.

Megan smiled. She had delivered one of her messages
successfully. But the other one was still in her hands. A
moment later, she handed the dispatch from General
Lafayette to Jeb Briggs. He looked carefully at both sides
of the paper and the writing on the front. "It is indeed
Lafayette's seal," he confirmed. Then he tucked the letter
into his belt. "The governor should return very soon, and
I'll give it to him the moment he arrives. It may contain
important information. I wish to thank you on his behalf,
Miss Ryder." He finished with a courteous bow.

The two soldiers who had captured Megan and Jason

looked deeply embarrassed. "Please accept our apology, miss," one began. "There are so many spies about, and Monticello has already been taken once."

"I've been masquerading as a boy, but let me assure you I'm not a Redcoat," she told them, smiling.

"Maybe not," Jason chimed in, "but you have as many secrets as a spy, Miss Ryder." He gave her a lopsided grin. "I'm delighted you're on our side. I wouldn't like to encounter a Redcoat with your fierce determination and bravery!"

Jeb Briggs insisted on sending Megan back to Wide Hall immediately with an escort and a note to his family. Megan gratefully accepted the ride.

As she climbed into the handsome black coach, she thanked Jason again for his help and wished him and Mr. Briggs good luck.

"Godspeed, Master Ryder," Jason replied warmly.

Mr. Briggs handed Megan a letter he'd hastily scrawled to his family and bade her farewell. At last the driver of the carriage gave the two white horses the signal to trot.

As Megan waved good-bye, she couldn't help feeling a little disappointed. After coming all this way, she hadn't gotten to meet Thomas Jefferson after all.

C h a p t e r
Eight

THE RETURN TRIP

The grounds at Wide Hall were illuminated by a full moon when Megan arrived. Hoping to slip into the house unseen, she convinced her escort to let her out at the gate. He wished her well, then drove on to Sue Ellen's house with the note from Jeb Briggs and another one from Megan telling Sue Ellen about her adventure. She smiled happily as she pictured Sue Ellen learning that her father was safe and that the message from General Lafayette had been delivered.

This time when Megan
entered the grand hallway,
it was completely empty.
She tiptoed upstairs to
retrieve her dress. She
peeled off the damp
clothes, hung them up on
the wooden peg where she
had found them, and slipped back
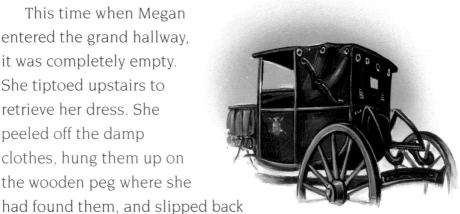
into her silky gown and dry shoes. A small
looking glass by the door was all she needed to wipe her
smudged face and fix her hair. As she brushed out the
grass and tangles, a sudden noise made her freeze.

A moment later, Megan realized that it was only Ellie,
closing the front door.

Megan was back in the attic.

She quickly removed the ball gown, carefully putting it
back in the trunk. As she picked up her great-
grandfather's book and headed for the stairs, she stole
one last glance at the black satin mask she had placed on
top of the neatly folded dress.

Her masquerade was over.

When Megan returned home, she heard her aunt
telling someone in the living room about her balloon ride.

Megan hurried into the room. "Dad!"

Her father opened his arms, and Megan raced into them. As he hugged her close, he noticed something tucked under her arm.

"That's Great Paul's book!" he exclaimed. "Is that what you were doing at Ellie's all day—reading your great-grandfather's book?"

"Uh . . . not exactly," Megan began, smiling. "But I was so excited when I saw it on the shelf, I asked Ellie if I could borrow it for awhile," she explained.

As they headed upstairs to freshen up for dinner, Megan told her father all about the time capsule. They sat down in her room to discuss it.

"So what's your artifact going to be?" he asked.

"I don't know," Megan confessed. "I haven't come up with anything yet."

Mr. Ryder pretended to look shocked. "Don't tell me my brilliant, talented, creative daughter doesn't have an idea."

"I've had a few ideas," Megan told him, "including a page from my diary. But I didn't think that would be important enough. I want my artifact to be something special—something that really helps kids understand the past. Do you know what I mean, Dad?"

"I think so," Mr. Ryder said thoughtfully. "I also think a page from your diary is a great idea."

"You do?" Megan sat on her bed as she thought it

over. "I like the idea of writing something," she mused, "but will anybody think my diary is interesting fifty years from now, or whenever our time capsule is found?"

Her father reached for Great Paul's book. "Why don't you take a look at this before making up your mind?"

Megan gave her father a quizzical look, but dutifully took the book from him. As she flipped through the pages, she saw that most of it was interviews her great-grandfather had done with people who lived through the Great Depression in America in the 1930s. He included hundreds of quotes from men, women, even children, all of them about how their families had been affected by the Depression.

Megan looked up. "I don't get it, Dad. This is interesting, but what does it have to do with me—or my diary?"

"A lot," her father replied. "Your diary is a record of our times, just like what those people said to Great Paul is a record of theirs."

But Megan still wasn't convinced. "My life isn't as exciting as yours, Dad," she pointed out. "I don't meet lots of famous people or get to watch important events in history, the way you do."

"History isn't only about famous people's lives, Megan," her father said gently. "That's something your great-grandfather told me when I was studying to be a journalist. And it's something I remember almost every single day on

my job, even when I'm covering big stories like the one in South America. History, he said, is about ordinary people leading ordinary lives."

Mr. Ryder stood up before Megan could reply. "It's getting late. Why don't you get changed and meet me downstairs in a few minutes. We can talk some more at dinner."

Megan nodded. But as her father left the room, Great Paul's words echoed in her head: History is about ordinary people leading ordinary lives.

Wasn't that what she'd just discovered on her adventure to the past? The Revolutionary War hadn't only been fought by big heroes like Thomas Jefferson and George Washington. People like Sue Ellen, Jason, and those wounded soldiers in the wagon, had made sacrifices, too. And their contributions were very important Megan realized, even if their names weren't mentioned in history books.

Megan was still lost in her thoughts as she crossed her room to the closet. But by the time she'd changed into her long, flowered skirt and the matching top, she'd made up her mind about something.

"Thank you, Great Paul," she whispered. Then she hurried down the stairs to tell her father what she had decided to put in the time capsule.

Diary

Dear Diary,

Today I'm writing a very special entry. It's for the lucky kids from the future who find the time capsule that my fifth-grade class buried in the schoolyard.

First, I want to introduce myself and tell you some things about me. My name is Megan Ryder and I'm eleven years old. I love to read all kinds of books, and to write. I might even become a writer or journalist when I grow up, but I'm not sure yet. Maybe I'll be famous by the time you find this time capsule, and you'll know what I decided to do for my career!

My parents are divorced and I live with my mom. Even though I don't get to see my dad very often, we're really close, especially since we both enjoy writing and reading so much.

I also want to tell you about my three best

friends. Their names are Keisha, Alison, and Heather. We spend a lot of time together doing things like listening to music, rollerblading, and just hanging out talking about everything from school to what's happening with our families. But probably the best thing we do together is visit our friend Ellie, and explore her attic. It's a wonderful, magical place, with all kinds of treasures. I wish I could tell you more about it, but it's our secret, and I've decided to let some of my secrets stay buried with the past!

Congratulations on finding our time capsule!

Sincerely,

Learn
More
About It

THE REVOLUTIONARY WAR

he Revolutionary War was a dramatic period in the history of the United States.

Great Britain had established itself as a worldwide empire, and by the middle of the eighteenth century its hold over the new colonies in America was weakening. The colonists grew increasingly angry at the British for imposing laws that dictated what they could and could not do, and yet they had no voice in the making of the laws. They became frustrated that Great Britain was getting very rich on the profits from their hard work. Also contributing to the colonists' unrest was the physical separation of the two nations—3,000 miles apart and divided by a great ocean. As a result, the colonists developed great self-reliance and required little from the empire across the sea.

The Revolutionary War began on April 19, 1775, when 800 British troops fought the colonial militia in what has become known as the Battle of Lexington and Concord. But it was a series of events that started years before, that set the stage for war.

The passage of the Tea Act in 1773 by British Parliament gave the East India Tea Company the right to determine who could sell tea—a very popular beverage of the colonists. Colonial merchants were angry. The new act meant that Parliament could eventually control all items that were sold in the colonies. The colonists' frustration led to the famous Boston Tea Party, where citizens dressed as Indians boarded three ships in Boston Harbor and dumped overboard hundreds of barrels of British-owned tea. In response, British ships formed a blockade around Boston Harbor. No ships were allowed to go in or out of Boston. This punishment hurt the colonists of Massachusetts, who relied on goods that came via the ships. The British intention was to starve the colonists until they repaid the cost of the dumped tea.

In Virginia, where Megan's adventure takes place, the call went out to all the colonies to create a new form of government—one that represented the colonists, not the king. The Continental Congress, an assembly of citizens from all walks of life, was held in Philadelphia, Pennsylvania, on September 1, 1774. It took two months of arguments and discussion, but the Congress, united in its efforts, resolved to boycott all British goods. The seeds for a revolution were already starting to bloom.

Paul Revere organized the Sons of Liberty, a group of colonial spies that monitored British activities. They were able to infiltrate the British ranks and learn information about planned attacks on the colonies. These rebel patriots were hailed as heroes, and many stories exist about their exploits.

As time passed, the talk of separation from Great Britain was growing stronger. In 1776, Thomas Paine wrote his famous essay *Common Sense*. In it, Paine criticized the government of England with its kings and queens. Royalty, he said, was the cause of many problems throughout the world. A person had to be born into a family in order to be a ruler, the person was not elected by the people. The vision that Paine had for the colonies demanded that the citizens believed absolutely in the power of freedom and independence—and that meant freedom and independence from Britain.

In 1781, while Megan was on her adventure at Monticello, British troops were assembling 125 miles southeast on the Virginia coast in Yorktown. The Redcoats, under the leadership of General Charles Cornwallis, were ordered to build a base for the Royal Navy. But 16,000 colonial troops, led in part by General

George Washington, surrounded the area. Cornwallis knew his troops were in trouble—they were sick from disease, hungry from lack of fresh food, and still suffering gravely from previous battle wounds. On October 19, Cornwallis surrendered. The surrender marked the end for the British hope of victory in America.

Megan's experiences during the American Revolution are a mixture of fact and fiction called "historical fiction." The historical events, including many of the figures and places described—Thomas Jefferson, Benedict Arnold, Banastre Tarleton, and Monticello—as well as the descriptions of the war and the attitude of the people are real. But they have been combined with other characters and situations that are fictional so that the story can be brought to life in an exciting way for the reader.

JOIN THE MAGIC ATTIC CLUB!

You can enjoy every adventure of the Magic Attic Club just by reading all the books. And there's more!

You can have a whole world of fun with the dolls, outfits, and accessories that are based on the books. And since Alison, Keisha, Heather, and Megan can wear one another's clothes, you can relive their adventures, or create new ones of your own!

To join the Magic Attic Club, just fill out this postcard and drop it in the mail, or call toll free **1-800-221-6972** We'll send you a **free** membership kit

including a poster, bookmark, postcards, and a catalog with all four dolls.

With your first purchase of a doll, you'll also receive your own key to the attic. And it's FREE!

Yes, I want to join the Magic Attic Club!

My name is _____

My address is _____

City _____ State _____ Zip _____

Birth date _____ Parent's Signature _____

955

And send a catalog to my friend, too!

My friend's name is _____

Address _____

City _____ State _____ Zip _____

956

If someone has already used the postcard from
this book and you would like a free Magic Attic Club
catalog, just send your full name and address to:

**Magic Attic Club
866 Spring Street
P.O. Box 9712
Portland, ME 04104-9954**

Or call toll free
1-800-775-9272

Code: 957

BUSINESS REPLY MAIL

FIRST-CLASS MAIL PERMIT NO. 8905 PORTLAND ME

POSTAGE WILL BE PAID BY THE ADDRESSEE

MAGIC ATTIC CLUB
866 SPRING ST
PO BOX 9712
PORTLAND ME   04104-9954